Adapted by David Lewman
Illustrated by Character Building and Fabio Laguna

🦢 A GOLDEN BOOK · NEW YORK

DreamWorks Trolls © 2016 DreamWorks Animation LLC. All Rights Reserved. Published in the
United States by Golden Books, an imprint of Random House Children's Books, a division of Penguin Random
House LLC, 1745 Broadway, New York, NY 10019, and in Canada by Penguin Random House Canada Limited,
Toronto, in conjunction with DreamWorks Animation LLC. Golden Books, A Golden Book, A Big Golden Book,
the G colophon, and the distinctive gold spine are registered trademarks of Penguin Random House LLC.
randomhousekids.com
ISBN 978-0-399-55895-5 (trade) — ISBN 978-0-399-55896-2 (ebook)
Printed in the United States of America
10 9 8 7 6 5 4 3 2 1

Once upon a time in a beautiful forest, there lived the happiest creatures the world has ever known . . . the **TROLLS**! They loved nothing more than to sing-sing-sing, dance-dance-dance, and hug-hug-hug all day long.

Unfortunately, the Trolls' boisterous singing attracted the
BERGENS—big, grumpy creatures who were always miserable.
And only one thing could make the Bergens happy . . .

EATING DELICIOUS TROLLS!

The Bergens chopped down almost all the trees in the forest to build **BERGEN TOWN**. They left just one tree for the Trolls and put a cage around it. Once a year, on a holiday they called **TROLLSTICE**, the Bergens gathered around the tree to eat Trolls. It was the one day they could actually *taste* happiness.

Young Prince Gristle couldn't wait for his very first Trollstice, when he would taste his very first Troll and finally experience happiness. But when Prince Gristle bit down on a Troll, all he tasted was wood! The Trolls were fake!

"WHERE DID THE DELICIOUS TROLLS GO?" roared his father, King Gristle.

Afraid of being eaten, the Trolls had dug tunnels under their tree and escaped from the Bergens. "We leave no Troll behind!" vowed their brave leader, King Peppy, carrying his Torch of Freedom. King Peppy helped every last Troll get away. He even carried his baby daughter, Poppy, hidden in his long hair! King Peppy led the Trolls to a wonderful forest home far away from the Bergens.

King Gristle was furious with the Royal Chef and blamed her for letting the Trolls escape. "You are hereby banished from Bergen Town!" he roared. "FOREVER!"

Prince Gristle asked his father what would make him happy now, since there were no Trolls to eat.

"Nothing," King Gristle answered miserably. "You will never, ever, EVER be happy!"

Many years later, after lots of singing, dancing, hugging, and scrapbooking, King Peppy's daughter, Poppy, was finally ready to lead the Trolls.

But before that, they needed to celebrate freedom from the Bergens! And that meant it was time for . . .

. . . THE BIGGEST, LOUDEST PARTY EVER!

All the Trolls were excited about the party except one worried
Troll named Branch.

"Your big, loud, crazy party is going to lead the Bergens straight to us!"
he warned. "They're out there somewhere—watching, waiting . . . listening!
While you make noise out here, I'll be in my highly camouflaged, heavily
fortified, Bergen-proof survival bunker!"

It had been a very long time since anyone had seen a Bergen, so the Trolls were tired of Branch's constant warnings. In fact, they were a little upset with him for spoiling their fun. But Creek, a calm and peaceful Troll, said Branch was just trying to help. "Branch WANTS to be miserable," Creek explained. "But I want ALL Trolls to be happy!" Poppy said.

At the celebration, all the Trolls (except Branch, of course) sang and danced. "Turn the music up!" Poppy called out. Grinning, DJ Suki pumped the music even louder. Poppy played along on her cowbell.

"MORE GLITTER!" Poppy shouted happily. The Trolls shined brightly colored spotlights into the sky. They fired the glitter cannons and set off a giant glitter explosion.

KaBOoOoM!!!!

Not too far away, in another part of the forest, the banished Royal Chef heard the explosions and thumping bass music. The alert Bergen peered through her spyglass and saw a burst of fireworks shaped like Poppy.

Could it be? she thought. *After all these years of searching, have I finally found . . .* THE TROLLS?

Chef stomped into Troll Village. BOOM! BOOM! BOOM!
"RUN!!!" Poppy yelled. The Trolls scattered, but Chef managed
to scoop up several of them—including Biggie, Mr. Dinkles, Smidge,
Cooper, Fuzzbert, Satin, Chenille, Guy Diamond, and Creek!

After Chef left, Poppy led the remaining Trolls to the safest place she could think of—Branch's underground bunker! She asked Branch to come with her to save her captured friends, but he thought that idea was even crazier than having a big, loud party in the first place!

"You're really going to Bergen Town on your own?" Branch asked when he realized what she was determined to do.

"My father didn't leave any Trolls behind, and neither will I," Poppy vowed.

The forest between the Trolls' home and Bergen Town turned out to be darker and more dangerous than Poppy had expected. Before she knew it, she found herself stuck in a big spiderweb! And to make matters worse, giant spiders were creeping out of the shadows.

BONK! One of the spiders got hit in the head with a frying pan! They turned around and saw Branch! Using his long hair like a whip—SNAP!—Branch drove the spiders off and rescued Poppy.

Poppy and Branch headed toward Bergen Town. As they made their way through the forest, Poppy sang to make herself feel better, but Branch only scowled.

"Maybe *you* should try singing," she suggested.

"I never sing," Branch stated firmly. "*Never.*"

They soon discovered a series of tunnels near the edge of Bergen Town.

"One of these tunnels leads to the Troll Tree," Poppy said.

"But the others lead to **CERTAIN DEATH**!" warned a talking cloud. Cloud Guy offered to show them the right tunnel, *if* . . . Branch would give him a high five! And a fist bump! And a hug! Branch got **SO** mad that he chased Cloud Guy, who led them all the way back to the old Troll Tree!

Meanwhile, in Bergen Town, Prince Gristle had grown up and become king. Hiding in the Troll Tree, Poppy and Branch watched worriedly as he displayed their Troll friends to the astonished Bergens. The newly un-banished Chef announced a Trollstice celebration the next night.

"That's right!" King Gristle crowed. "Happiness is back on the menu!"

In the Bergens' castle, Poppy and Branch snuck down a chandelier to spy on King Gristle. He was trying on his old Trollstice bib, which was way too tight. **RRRIP!**

When Cooper giggled, King Gristle realized there weren't enough Trolls for a Trollstice celebration. To calm the angry king down, Chef popped Creek into his mouth!

King Gristle left the dining room with Creek in his mouth. Chef turned to the scullery maid and barked, "Bridget, lock these Trolls in your room and guard them with your miserable little life!"

As Bridget wheeled the Trolls away in their cage, Poppy jumped onto one of her apron strings. Branch had no choice but to do the same!

Once inside Bridget's room, Poppy saw that the walls were covered with pictures of King Gristle. Bridget lay on her bed, sobbing. *She's in* **LØVE** *with him!* Poppy thought. Poppy convinced the lovesick Bergen to help her rescue her friends by promising to help her win the king's love with a new outfit and a new hairdo!

While King Gristle was shopping at Bibbly Bibbington's Bibs, Bridget walked into the store with the Trolls atop her head. They were using their magical hair to create a rainbow-colored wig. Impressed by her beauty, the king asked her name. Repeating after the hidden Trolls, she answered, "Lady Glittersparkles."

King Gristle asked her on a date right then and there!

King Gristle and Bridget had a great time eating pizza and talking. With Poppy and Branch in her wig, whispering all the right things to say into her ears, Bridget captivated King Gristle. Then Bridget spoke from her heart: "Being here with you today makes me realize that true happiness *is* possible."

"It is," the king agreed, opening his locket to reveal Creek. He was still alive! "True happiness is a lot closer than you think."

After dinner, King Gristle and Bridget roller-skated together. As the two Bergens zoomed around the rink, the Trolls in Bridget's wig held on for dear life. King Gristle liked Lady Glittersparkles so much that he invited her to be his guest at the Trollstice feast.

"YES!" Bridget agreed, thrilled.

Suddenly, Chef interrupted their date. She eyed Lady Glittersparkles suspiciously. Worried that she would be recognized, Bridget hurried away, dropping one roller skate.

"I'll see you at Trollstice, Lady Glittersparkles!" King Gristle called after her, picking up her skate and holding it tenderly.

Back in her room, Bridget was happy—until she saw the Trolls leaving to rescue Creek. "No, no!" she cried. "You have to help me be Lady Glittersparkles. I need you!"

"But you can't pretend to be someone you're not forever," Poppy said as they left to save Creek. Bridget threw herself on her bed and sobbed.

Meanwhile, in his bedroom, King Gristle got on his treadmill. He wanted to be in good shape for his next date with Lady Glittersparkles. The Trolls snuck into the bedroom and snatched the locket. But King Gristle's pet alligator spotted them!

The Trolls sped through the castle on a roller skate.
"Hold on!" Poppy yelled. The scaly pet chased them, snapping
his massive jaws full of razor-sharp teeth.

They finally escaped into the kitchen, where Poppy noticed
that Creek wasn't in the locket! "Where'd he go?" she cried
as—WHAM!—Chef slammed a cage down over the Trolls!

Chef sneered. "Creek is going to lead me to the rest of the Trolls!"
Poppy couldn't believe it, but Creek admitted he'd sold out his
fellow Trolls to save himself from being eaten.

"Believe me, I wish there were some other way, but there isn't,"
Creek said, reaching through the bars of the cage to take Poppy's
cowbell out of her hair.

Creek went back to the Trolls' deserted village and rang the cowbell.

"It's Poppy's cowbell!" King Peppy cried happily. "She's come back with the others!"

The Trolls rushed out of Branch's bunker . . . only to be gathered up by Chef and her guards!

Back in the castle's kitchen, Chef tossed all the Trolls into a big cooking pot. "I failed," Poppy said miserably. "I got everyone I love thrown in a pot."

All the color drained out of her. But then Branch started singing. (**YES, BRANCH!**) He sang about showing your true colors. And then something amazing happened: *his* true colors came out! Poppy was filled with joy and sang along with Branch. Then her colors returned, too!

"Well," Poppy said, "we danced and hugged and sang. Now what?"
The lid was lifted off the pot. It was Bridget! "Now . . . you get
out of here!" she said. She'd heard Branch's beautiful song and just
couldn't let the Trolls be eaten. "Go! Now!"

The Trolls ran off through the tunnels. But then Poppy stopped.
She felt sorry for Bridget, and for all the Bergens who'd never
gotten to be happy.

At the Trollstice feast, Bridget admitted that she had let the Trolls go. As Chef was about to have her arrested, the Trolls stormed into the banquet hall on a roller skate! They jumped onto Bridget's head and formed themselves into the rainbow wig.

"Lady Glittersparkles?" King Gristle cried, amazed. He realized that when they were together, he was HAPPY even WITHOUT eating a Troll.

Poppy told the Bergens that all they needed to be happy was to hug and sing and dance! Poppy and Branch started singing and dancing, and soon everyone joined in. They all felt happy! (Except Chef, who was ejected from the castle.)

"They've changed our point of view through the power of song and dance!" one Bergen said. King Gristle and Bridget could not have agreed more.

Back in their village, the Trolls kept the party going. King Peppy passed Poppy the Torch of Freedom and placed a crown on her head, announcing, "Our new queen!"

AND THEY ALL LIVED VERY HAPPILY EVER AFTER . . .
EVEN THE BERGENS!